THE COUNTRY NOISY BOOK

by Margaret Wise Brown

pictures by Leonard Weisgard

HarperCollins*Publishers*

Once there was a little dog named Muffin.

When the days were hot Muffin's family all went to the country.

We're off to the country, they said.

And you are going to the country, too, Muffin, for the first time in your life.

Only you are going there in a box.

chug chug chug chug chug chugchugchug

Then Muffin's family got into the airplane where dogs couldn't go. And they flew right over Muffin's train on their way to the country. Muffin could hear the far-off

Drrrrrrr Brrrrrrrrrrrrrrrrrrrrrrrr

But he did not know that was an airplane with his family in it.

All night on the train Muffin heard

Clickety clack clickety clack
Pocketa pocketa pocketa pocketa
Clickety clack clickety clack

He wondered what it was.

In the morning the train stopped somewhere.

Cocka doodle doo

What was that!

Chirp Chirp Chirp

What was that!

Baa Baa Baa

What was that!

Moo Moo Moo

What was that!

Bow wow wow

Muffin knew what that was.

Then they put Muffin's box with Muffin in it on a boat. Muffin's family were waiting for him across the river. Muffin sat in his box. He couldn't see where he was going. But Muffin could hear

Clank clank clank clink clank
Ding dong
Swish swish

Feet were walking by, and the boat was shaking. And Muffin could smell a fishy smell.

When they came to the shore, Muffin's box
was carried off the boat. And, all of a sudden,
Muffin smelled his family.
And he heard

>Why here is that little dog Muffin
>
>Open the box
>
>Quick
>
>Kerchew

And out jumped Muffin
And there was his family
And there was Muffin in the country.

At first it seemed very quiet. Then he heard

Caw Caw Caw

What was that!

Bzzzzz Bzzzzz

What was that!

Honky Donky onk onk onk

What was that!

Chip chop Chip chop chop chop chop

What was that!

Quack quack Quack quack

What was that!

Cheee Cheeeeee Cheeeeee

What was that!

Peck peck peck peck

What was that!

Gobble Gobble Gobble

What was that!

Then he heard little noises
        Crickets
            ticka ticka ticka ticka
        Mosquitoes
            ? . . . . ?
        A little bird flying
            ? . . . . ?
        A butterfly
            ? . . . . ?
        The wind
            ? . . . . ?

Then it was night
and the stars came out.

Could Muffin hear that?

**All around in the country it was dark
And Muffin began to hear the night noises**

Whoo

    Whooo

Whoo

    Whooo

What was that!

Whip poor Will

Whip poor Will

Whip poor Will

What was that!

Katydid

    Katydidn't

    Katydid

      Katydidn't

What was that!

All through the long grasses and in the trees there were little lights flashing on and off, little bug lights.

Wink

    Wink

        Wink went the lightning bugs

But could Muffin hear that?

Flap

Flap

Flap

What was that!

Then a skunk went by without a sound.

Muffin walked past the pig pen

Umph

Umph

Umph

What was that!

eek

eeeeek

eeeeeek

What was that!

Then Muffin took a walk into the night
And he walked past the frog pond

Jugarum

Jugarum

Jugarum

What was that!

Then Muffin was sleepy, so he went back into the house.
All was quiet except for a

tick tock tick tock tick tock tick tock
cuckoo!   cuckoo!

Then he heard a soft

Prrrrrrrrrrr Prrrrrrrrrrrrr
Prrrrrrrrrrrrrrrrrrrrr

What could that be?

It was a soft little pussycat, warm and sleepy. And Muffin curled up with the soft little pussycat.

And then Muffin fell asleep and he didn't hear any more noises.

Not even the wind.